MR. SNEEZE

by Roger Hargreaves

This is Coldland, which is a country somewhere near the North Pole.

The weather in Coldland is winter all the time. When it isn't snowing it's freezing and when it isn't freezing it's snowing, so you can imagine how cold it is.

Because it's so cold in Coldland, everybody who lives there is cold as well.

You can tell if somebody comes from Coldland because everybody there has a red nose.

And people in Coldland aren't the only ones with red noses. In Coldland you can see red-nosed dogs chasing red-nosed cats chasing red-nosed mice.

In Coldland you can even see red-nosed elephants!

And what you hear most of the time in Coldland is a noise that sounds like this.

The sound of the sneeze is very common indeed in Coldland.

Which is not very surprising, is it?

This is the story of Mr Sneeze, who lived in a small snow-covered cottage in Shivertown, the capital of Coldland.

Every morning Mr Sneeze woke up, sneezed, got up, sneezed, got dressed, sneezed, went downstairs, sneezed, ate his breakfast, sneezed, and went to work, still sneezing.

"I don't like this sneezing all the time," he thought to himself every day, until one day he decided to leave Coldland and try to find a cure for the sneezes.

So that very same day Mr Sneeze packed the things he'd need for his journey (mainly handkerchiefs), sneezed, locked his front door, sneezed, and set off.

He walked and sneezed and sneezed and walked his way across Coldland, and then he sneezed and walked and walked and sneezed for days and days until Coldland was far behind.

As he walked away from Coldland he noticed that there was less and less snow. And eventually he walked so far that there was no snow at all.

And as he walked, he noticed something else. He wasn't walking and sneezing, he was walking and walking.

For the first time in his life he wasn't sneezing.

Not at all. Not a bit. Not even the tiniest tishoo.

"I wonder why I'm not sneezing?" he thought to himself.

But he must have thought his thought out loud to himself, because a voice behind him replied, "You're not sneezing because you haven't got a cold."

Mr Sneeze jumped, turned, and there behind him stood a wise old wizard.

"What's a cold?" asked Mr Sneeze.

"A cold is what you catch when you're too cold," said the wise old wizard, wisely.

"Oh," said Mr Sneeze. "But I come from a country called Coldland where everybody is too cold all the time!"

"Nonsense," snorted the wizard. "It can't be too cold *all* the time because of the sun," and he pointed to the sun, which was smiling in the sky.

"But we don't have any sun in Coldland," said Mr Sneeze.

"No sun!" exclaimed the wizard. "How extremely extraordinarily extraordinary. We'd better do something about that then, hadn't we?"

"Yes," agreed Mr Sneeze, not quite knowing what the wizard was talking about.

"How far away is this place called Coldland?" asked the wizard.

"Oh, it's miles and miles and miles away," replied Mr Sneeze.

"In which direction?" asked the wizard.

Mr Sneeze pointed.

"Shouldn't take long," said the wizard, who then waved his wand and muttered some magic words, which wouldn't be magic if we told you what they were.

Whatever those magic words were, they worked.

Before you could say "Sneeze" both the wizard and Mr Sneeze were transported to Shivertown, which you will remember is the capital of Coldland.

As usual it was snowing.

"I say, this is a cold, gloomy place," said the wizard.

"Atishoo!" replied Mr Sneeze, who had started sneezing again.

"Coldland certainly needs some sunshine," said the wizard. "And that's going to take some rather special magic."

"Please hurry up," said Mr Sneeze, who was rapidly turning into a snowman.

"Now," said the wizard, ignoring him. "I'm going to say some magic words, and I want you to sneeze three times immediately afterwards."

The wise old wizard then held up his magic wand and muttered some more magic words, which again wouldn't be magic if we told you what they were.

"Atishoo! Atishoo! Atishoo!" sneezed Mr Sneeze.

Then quite suddenly, as if by magic, which indeed it was, the sun came out from behind the big black clouds.

And it stopped snowing.

"There now," said the wizard. "That should stop the sneezing."

And then, after muttering some more magic words, and without waiting to even say goodbye, he disappeared.

Mr Sneeze just stood there in the sunshine, watching the snow begin to melt.

After that the sun shone every day, and today Coldland isn't anything like it used to be.

You can't see red-nosed dogs chasing red-nosed cats chasing red-nosed mice any more.

And these days, the sound of the sneeze is a very uncommon sound indeed.

And even Mr Sneeze doesn't sneeze any more.

And that isn't the only thing different about Mr Sneeze, as he discovered himself when he looked in the mirror one morning.

Can you see what was different about Mr Sneeze?

It happened one other time too.

See if you can find the page where that was!

3 Great Offers for MR.MEN Fans!

MR.MEN TOKEN

1 New Mr. Men or Little Miss Library Bus Presentation Cases

A brand new stronger, roomier school bus library box, with sturdy carrying handle and stay-closed fasteners.
The full colour, wipe-clean boxes make a great home for your full collection.
They're just £5.99 inc P&P and free bookmark!

☐ MR. MEN ☐ LITTLE MISS (please tick and order overleaf)

2 Door Hangers and Posters

In every Mr. Men and Little Miss book like this one, you will find a special token. Collect 6 tokens and we will send you a brilliant Mr. Men or Little Miss poster and a Mr. Men or Little Miss double sided full colour bedroom door hanger of your choice. Simply tick your choice in the list and tape a 50p coin for your two items to this page.

PLEASE STICK YOUR 50P COIN HERE

Door Hangers (please tick)
☐ Mr. Nosey & Mr. Muddle
☐ Mr. Slow & Mr. Busy
☐ Mr. Messy & Mr. Quiet
☐ Mr. Perfect & Mr. Forgetful
☐ Little Miss Fun & Little Miss Late
☐ Little Miss Helpful & Little Miss Tidy
☐ Little Miss Busy & Little Miss Brainy
☐ Little Miss Star & Little Miss Fun

Posters (please tick)
☐ MR.MEN
☐ LITTLE MISS

3 Sixteen Beautiful Fridge Magnets – any 2 for £2.00! inc.P&P

They're very special collector's items!
Simply tick your first and second* choices from the list below
of any 2 characters!

1st Choice

- [ ] Mr. Happy
- [ ] Mr. Lazy
- [ ] Mr. Topsy-Turvy
- [ ] Mr. Bounce
- [ ] Mr. Bump
- [ ] Mr. Small
- [ ] Mr. Snow
- [ ] Mr. Wrong

- [ ] Mr. Daydream
- [ ] Mr. Tickle
- [ ] Mr. Greedy
- [ ] Mr. Funny
- [ ] Little Miss Giggles
- [ ] Little Miss Splendid
- [ ] Little Miss Naughty
- [ ] Little Miss Sunshine

2nd Choice

- [ ] Mr. Happy
- [ ] Mr. Lazy
- [ ] Mr. Topsy-Turvy
- [ ] Mr. Bounce
- [ ] Mr. Bump
- [ ] Mr. Small
- [ ] Mr. Snow
- [ ] Mr. Wrong

- [ ] Mr. Daydream
- [ ] Mr. Tickle
- [ ] Mr. Greedy
- [ ] Mr. Funny
- [ ] Little Miss Giggles
- [ ] Little Miss Splendid
- [ ] Little Miss Naughty
- [ ] Little Miss Sunshine

*Only in case your first choice is out of stock.

--- TO BE COMPLETED BY AN ADULT ---

To apply for any of these great offers, ask an adult to complete the coupon below and send it with the appropriate payment and tokens, if needed, to MR. MEN OFFERS, PO BOX 7, MANCHESTER M19 2HD

- [ ] Please send ____ Mr. Men Library case(s) and/or ____ Little Miss Library case(s) at £5.99 each inc P&P
- [ ] Please send a poster and door hanger as selected overleaf. I enclose six tokens plus a 50p coin for P&P
- [ ] Please send me ____ pair(s) of Mr. Men/Little Miss fridge magnets, as selected above at £2.00 inc P&P

Fan's Name _____

Address _____

_____ **Postcode** _____

Date of Birth _____

Name of Parent/Guardian _____

Total amount enclosed £_____

- [ ] I enclose a cheque/postal order payable to Egmont Books Limited
- [ ] Please charge my MasterCard/Visa/Amex/Switch or Delta account (delete as appropriate)

| | | | | | | | | | | | | | | | | | | Card Number

Expiry date ___/___ **Signature** _____

Please allow 28 days for delivery. Offer is only available while stocks last. We reserve the right to change the terms of this offer at any time and we offer a 14 day money back guarantee. This does not affect your statutory rights. Data Protection Act: If you do not wish to receive other similar offers from us or companies we recommend, please tick this box [ ]. Offers apply to UK only.

MR.MEN   LITTLE MISS
Mr. Men and Little Miss™ & ©Mrs. Roger Hargreaves